SandCastle

Compound Words

bed + time =
bedtime

Amanda Rondeau

Consulting Editor Monica Marx, M.A./Reading Specialist

ABDO
Publishing Company

Published by SandCastle™, an imprint of ABDO Publishing Company, 4940 Viking Drive, Edina, Minnesota 55435.

Credits
Edited by: Pam Price
Curriculum Coordinator: Nancy Tuminelly
Cover and Interior Design and Production: Mighty Media
Photo Credits: Comstock, Hemera, PhotoDisc, Rubberball Productions, Stockbyte

Library of Congress Cataloging-in-Publication Data

Rondeau, Amanda, 1974-
    Bed + time = bedtime / Amanda Rondeau.
      p. cm. -- (Compound words)
    Includes index.
    Summary: Illustrations and easy-to-read text introduce compound words related to family and home.
    ISBN 1-59197-431-3
    1. English language--Compound words--Juvenile literature. [1. English language--Compound words.] I. Title: Bed plus time equals bedtime. II. Title.

PE1175.R665 2003
428.1--dc21

                                                                        2003048008

SandCastle™ books are created by a professional team of educators, reading specialists, and content developers around five essential components that include phonemic awareness, phonics, vocabulary, text comprehension, and fluency. All books are written, reviewed, and leveled for guided reading, early intervention reading, and Accelerated Reader® programs and designed for use in shared, guided, and independent reading and writing activities to support a balanced approach to literacy instruction.

Let Us Know

After reading the book, SandCastle would like you to tell us your stories about reading. What is your favorite page? Was there something hard that you needed help with? Share the ups and downs of learning to read. We want to hear from you! To get posted on the ABDO Publishing Company Web site, send us e-mail at:

sandcastle@abdopub.com

SandCastle Level: Transitional

A compound word is two words joined together to make a new word.

bed + time =

bedtime

Sue's mom reads
a story at bedtime.

book + shelf =

bookshelf

Joe finds a good book on the bookshelf in the library.

fire + place =

fireplace

Greg and Carol have a fireplace in their new house.

week + end =

weekend

Nick and his dad play soccer on the weekend.

bed + room =

bedroom

Amy and Debbie
are sisters.
They share a
bedroom.

drive + way =

driveway

Maggie helps her dad wash the car in the driveway.

Good Morning at Bedtime

We call our grandpa Willy.

He says good night at breakfast and good morning at bedtime.

Isn't he silly!

His driveway is the only one in town that is round.

And when you ring his doorbell,
you hear a chirping sound!

His bathroom is like an art museum.

We always have fun when we go
to see him.

More Compound Words

carport	headboard
clothesline	keyhole
cupboard	kinfolk
doorknob	livingroom
doorway	overnight
grandchild	wallpaper
grandma	washcloth
grandparents	

Glossary

bedtime   the time that you usually go to bed

bookshelf   a shelf for holding books

driveway   a private road that goes from the street to a house or garage

fireplace   a stone, brick, or metal structure in which a fire is burned

museum   a place where important objects are studied and displayed

About SandCastle™

A professional team of educators, reading specialists, and content developers created the SandCastle™ series to support young readers as they develop reading skills and strategies and increase their general knowledge. The SandCastle™ series has four levels that correspond to early literacy development in young children. The levels are provided to help teachers and parents select the appropriate books for young readers.

Emerging Readers
(no flags)

Beginning Readers
(1 flag)

Transitional Readers
(2 flags)

Fluent Readers
(3 flags)

These levels are meant only as a guide. All levels are subject to change.

ABDO
Publishing Company

To see a complete list of SandCastle™ books and other nonfiction titles from ABDO Publishing Company, visit www.abdopub.com or contact us at:

4940 Viking Drive, Edina, Minnesota 55435 • 1-800-800-1312 • fax: 1-952-831-1632